Give Thanks
for Each Day

by **Steve Metzger**
illustrated by
Robert McPhillips

Cartwheel
·B·O·O·K·S·®

SCHOLASTIC INC.

New York   Toronto   London   Auckland   Sydney   Mexico City   New Delhi   Hong Kong

To Krebs – S.M.

I give thanks for Sam and Silkie Sue. – R.M.

Text copyright © 2011 by Steve Metzger.
Illustrations copyright © 2011 by Robert McPhillips.

All rights reserved. Published by Scholastic Inc.
SCHOLASTIC, CARTWHEEL BOOKS, and associated logos are trademarks and/or registered trademarks of Scholastic Inc.

ISBN 978-0-545-34967-3

10 9 8 7 6 5 4   12 13 14 15

First printing, September 2011
Designed by Angela Jun

Give thanks for each day. Give thanks for each night.

For colorful flowers,
For stars shining bright.

Give thanks for new crayons,
Red, green, and blue.

Give thanks for the moments
When wishes come true.

Give thanks for the train
That chugs down the track.

Give thanks for the comfort

When Mommy comes back.

Give thanks for a puzzle,
A favorite bear.

The thrill when you're lifted
Way up in the air.

A hug! A parade!

A bath! A new toy!

The things in our world
That fill us with joy!

Give thanks for a walk
By a lake in the park.

Give thanks for the light
In our home after dark.

Give thanks for the snowflakes
That fall from above.

For getting together
With people you love.

Give thanks for sweet ice cream,

For ducks in a row.

Give thanks for great stories,
Which help you to grow.

Give thanks for the ocean.
Give thanks for the sand.

The sweet, simple pleasure
When we're holding hands.

Give thanks for "I love you,"

The best words to say.

Give thanks for each night. Give thanks for each day.